Right Click, Love

a novella by

M.B. Feeney

M.B. Feeney

Praise for Right Click, Love

"A well-rounded, fun and topical view on today's world of modern romance, *Right Click, Love* sees our two single characters set up a blog to post about their dating experiences. From the moment I read the first paragraph, I was hooked...not only on the idea behind the story, but on the characters, and their not always quite successful experiences in the dating world. It made me realize how the dating scene has not become easier, but in fact is probably more complicated than ever. M.B. Feeney has a style that is entertaining, funny, and unique with its British flavor and well-rounded characters. I can't wait to see what she comes up with next. Great read."

~ author LJ Harris *Heart of Glass*

"...this book was a pleasure to read from the proverbial cover to cover. I loved the characters, the plot, the humour, just everything. I'm hard to please, but this was just perfect for a short, sharp burst of laughter and happiness after a tough day. It's firmly stored in my 'Favourites' folder on the kindle, and I can see it being one I read over and over again. I honestly cannot recommend it highly enough, particularly if you are a fan of a witty and realistic type of romance with a twist."

~Lily Loves Indie

3

M.B. Feeney

Right Click, Love

M.B. Feeney

Acknowledgments

Firstly, Mavvy, Rachel, and Tammy. Thank you all
for holding my hand through this 2nd edition. It is
because of you it not only looks amazing, but I
finally am able to say it is mine.

To everyone who has supported me over the last
two years, I am amazed. I never expected the
responses I've had. You humble me.

To anyone who has bought this book. It may be
short, and it may be fluffy, I just hope you enjoy it
and maybe tell a friend.

Dedication

This is one for anyone who has been on a bad date,
and to those that knew from date one.

Table of Contents

Chapter One: Why Would You? 10

Chapter Two: The Clock's Ticking 17

Chapter 3: Romance with a Hint of Scrutiny 26

Chapter Four: Bowling for Soup 33

Chapter Five: Take a Chance 40

Chapter Six: Back in the Game 48

Chapter Seven: Next Time, Call a Decorator 55

Chapter Eight: Is 'The Chase' Worth It? 62

Chapter Nine: Do My High Street Bargains Offend You? 69

Chapter Ten: To Quote Cher: 'If I Could Turn Back Time' 77

Chapter Eleven: Meet the Parents 85

Chapter Twelve: Return of the Mack......................92

Chapter Thirteen: What to Expect When You're Not Expecting 99

Chapter Fourteen: Honesty is the Best Policy 107

Chapter 15: It's Not Goodbye — It's See You Later 114

Epilogue: There's a Light at the End of the Tunnel 122

About the Author 132

Right Click, Love

Chapter One: Why Would You?

Sipping her hot coffee, Jodie Lynch tapped in her login details to check how well the latest blog post had been received. The stats were through the roof, and there were almost thirty comments awaiting approval. She'd never expected that writing about the non-existent sex life being experienced by her and her best friend Louise Hewson would garner so much attention.

Ever since they'd started the blog six months ago, after suffering yet another dire date with someone who wasn't what they'd 'advertised,' the friends had begun to enjoy the torture of dating. Back then, Jodie had sat with Louise, drinking cheap rosé into the early hours and lamenting the lack of decent, single, honest men who still had their own hair and teeth. That wasn't too much to ask, was it? Without thinking and under the influence, Jodie had pulled out her laptop and set up the blog. She'd been thankful that she hadn't posted anything that evening, and she had almost deleted the blog altogether once she'd overcome her hangover the next day. However, after speaking with Louise, Jodie had decided to go ahead with the no-holds-barred outlet for their frustration.

She read the last post back before looking at the comments.

~*~*~

14 June 2012 - Why Would You?

So, Louise got set up on another blind date by her boss Theresa. She kept telling Louise that Mark was "such a nice guy" and "so perfect for you." Since pickings had been slim, Lou tarted herself up, yet again making me jealous of her gorgeous, slim, petite figure, which made my almost six-foot frame look extra gangly. As I curled her hair, she began her age-old whining about wanting my red hair. Who wants to be ginger with all the hassle

11

we get? Anyway, I digress. She got ready and went to meet him at the local Bella Pasta (his choice, not hers. *eye roll*). Typical Louise, she arrived early. She decided to wait at the tiny bar and get herself a drink — non-alcoholic, of course, since we ALL know what happened last time. While she waited, she scoped out all the escape points. Just in case.

She waited and waited and waited. Just as Lou was about to leave, Mark showed up, full of apologies and clutching what looked rather like a bunch of wilting, petrol station carnations. Against her better judgment, she decided to stay because she was more than a little hungry and pretty much past caring about what company she had.

In the short amount of time between ordering and her meal's arrival in front of her, she realised that Mark was not the guy for her. He wasn't even the guy for now. They had NOTHING in common. I mean, who the hell hasn't heard of Nirvana? That right there was a deal breaker for Lou, not to mention he was shy to the point of being mute. She ate — fast — and then made a dash

for the ladies' to send me an SOS
text.

It was unlucky for Lou that I was
working late and my phone was on
silent, in my bag, locked away in my
filing cabinet. I didn't get the
message until an hour and a half
later. By that time, she had been
escorted to her front door by Mark,
who was angling for an invite inside
for "coffee."

When I managed to call her, she'd
barricaded herself in her flat and had
drunk almost half a bottle of brandy
to purge the memory of yet another
shitty date. I made my way over as
soon as I finished work, knowing that
if I didn't, I'd never escape the
phone calls and texts informing me how
I had failed in my duty as a best
friend. The rest of the night was not
pretty.

~*~*~

Jodie couldn't help but laugh at the memory of

the state Louise had been in. When she'd let

herself into the flat, her best friend had been

13

trembling with shock and anger at how the meek Mark had transformed into an octopus during the walk home. What had begun with him walking a little too close had ended with him trying to get more than a simple goodnight kiss. Much more, in fact, which had forced Louise to resort to a swift knee in the balls and to leg it inside before he could register the agony of what she had done. Her brown eyes were bloodshot from the amount of alcohol she'd managed to sink in the time between her call and Jodie's arrival.

"So, her search continues, as does mine," was the closing line of the post, and it depressed Jodie slightly. *How hard could it be to find a decent guy in London?* She saw it happening all the time to her other friends and work colleagues. They met; they had fun; they got married, had kids, and mostly more or less lived happy ever after. Had she pissed someone off so much that they had marked her card as "single forever?"

Both Jodie and Louise had always prided themselves on their ability to not define themselves by their relationships or the men they dated, casual or not. They weren't the kind of women who needed a man in their lives to feel complete or whole, but it was still ridiculous how hard it was not letting a lack of "happy ever after" get you down.

The comments under the post made her smile. The majority were from regular readers who, she knew, were having similar experiences. Other readers felt as if they had settled for the first available guy that had shown them the slightest bit of interest, and were now living the lives of their mothers. These women had emailed the pair of them on numerous occasions to offer support, friendship, and love, which amazed Jodie and

Louise both. Neither one of them would have expected such an outpouring of camaraderie from women they had never met. The men who read the blog . . . they weren't always as accepting of what was written. Well, not the straight ones anyway. The blog's numerous gay male followers thought it was fantastic that they were having the same problems finding a man as the women were.

A couple of the men they had dated had caught wind of posts on the blog and were far from impressed with what had been written about them. However, since everything was true, they never tried to get anything removed. Also, Jodie and Louise were both careful to ensure privacy. They never used surnames or gave out location details; it was simple common sense, which allowed them to not only avoid any grief they might get, but also a possible lawsuit.

Chapter Two: The Clock's Ticking

Jodie let herself into her flat after a long day of mind-numbing meetings. She collapsed onto her sofa for a few minutes, thanking every deity she knew for the fact that it was Friday.

Under normal circumstances, she loved her job as a legal secretary, but all-day depositions always drained her. Days like that were bad enough any day of the week, but on a Friday, were just cruel and unusual torture. Audio transcription and shorthand became a dim memory once she'd opened a bottle of chilled wine. Glass in hand, she rummaged through drawers for her well-used take away menus.

"Hey, where are thee?" Louise's voice floated through the small flat when she let herself in an hour later with the spare key.

Without moving from the kitchen table, Jodie poured another glass of wine and slid it across the table, waiting for Louise to join her.

"Kitchen." Jodie shook the stack of glossy menus as Louise joined her. "What do you fancy tonight?"

"We haven't had Chinese for a few weeks. Oh, I have my own leaflet." Louise handed Jodie a matte black sheet with shocking pink lettering that spelled out: Speed dating, 8-10pm @ The Prince of Wales every 3rd Saturday.

"Where did you get this?" Jodie poured two more glasses of wine after ordering their food, handed one to Louise, then led the way into the lounge.

"It was stuck to one of the maps at the tube station this morning. What do you think?"

"I think we need to sort out what to wear."
Jodie scanned her wardrobe in her head while she
sipped her wine.

~*~*~

23 June 2012 — The Clock's ticking

I use the tube every day, like many
others, so why do I feel it necessary
to look at the map every bloody
morning? Well, this time the map was
obscured by about ten glossy, black
leaflets that had been stuck all over
it. At first I didn't take any notice,
but I soon did when I saw the fetching
pink writing (see scanned picture
attached). I realised that I needed to
keep it to show Jodie. After I'd
snagged one, I also realised they were
every-bloody-where. It was if they
were taunting me.

I admit that I've always looked at
speed dating as a bit of a joke. It's
always used in RomCom films. When the
female lead is getting a bit
desperate, her bestie takes her for a
night out surrounded by fellas and
booze. The usual outcome is an evening

19

of hilarity and drunken frolics. It
sometimes ends in a disastrous one-
night stand, which helps to remind
said female lead who she's in love
with or scares the male lead into
thinking that the female lead has
moved on. *Et voila*, happy ever after.
Speed dating on TV and in films ends
in the same way; it is such a huge
disaster that it causes said female
lead . . . see above plotline for the
rest. Anything goes to get the two
leads into each other's arms for a
happy ever after.

So, naturally, Jodie and I are going
to check it out — just for "research
purposes," you understand. Neither of
us expects anything to come from it;
we're going with an open mind and the
appetite for a good time. Neither of
us is that lucky, but what have we got
to lose?

Check back in a couple of days for our
report.

~*~*~

Jodie sat back giggling as she watched Louise
publish her post.

"This is going to be a complete nightmare. You do realise that, don't you?" Jodie slurred her words when she spoke.

Louise turned and looked her in the eye. "It may well be, but we have to explore this avenue of research. Next step is online dating."

That particular prospect scared the living daylights out of the both of them, considering the bad rap it had been given by the media regarding the apparent number of sexual predators combing the net for their next victim.

~*~

The pub wasn't far, which allowed them to walk. Heels clacking on the bone-dry pavement, Jodie and Louise clutched each other's arms for support.

"It's times like this that I wish I'd never quit smoking." Louise fumbled in her bag for a packet of gum. Jodie hadn't seen her friend so nervous in a long time, but she wasn't feeling all that calm herself. She didn't do well with being thrust into situations in which she had to sell herself. It was bad enough doing so on a one-to-one basis during a date over a few hours; she couldn't begin to fathom how to do it in just a few minutes. Maybe they could find somewhere else to go and just go on the pull like normal women in their late twenties. Jodie was just about to suggest this to Louise when they arrived. They hovered outside the open door for a couple of seconds before Louise gathered her confidence and took charge, dragging Jodie inside and straight to the bar.

Both women felt better at once with a glass of wine in their hands; so much so that they dug up the courage to join the queue at the registration desk. It was a surprise to find out that they had to complete an information sheet.

"They do realise we're not signing up for a dating agency, don't they?" There was a slight hint of panic to Louise's voice as they handed back their completed forms to the bored-looking hostess. Each received a "Hello, my name is. . ." sticker before they were led to small tables, each featuring a candle for atmosphere, and a notepad and a pencil for taking notes.

"Way to create an atmosphere. Romance with just a hint of scrutiny." Jodie laughed without humour as she looked around the room at the other women who had already been seated.

"Ooh. I like that quote. Will work well on the blog." Jodie watched as Louise scribbled the words down on a piece of paper before folding it and slotting it in her pocket. She rolled her eyes as Louise lifted her glass in thanks.

~*~

They found to their delight that the evening wasn't a complete waste of time. After the event was over and they had handed in their sheets detailing anyone they might have interest in, both women got half a dozen or so back.

"These are yours to do with as you wish. Each gentleman has an email address that routes via our offices if you wish to contact them at a later date," the hostess explained to them before thanking them for their participation.

"Will you contact anyone?" Louise asked as they made their way back to her flat, which was the closest.

"I don't know right now. I need to go over my notes." A typical secretary, Jodie had made notes on each three-minute encounter, listing likes and dislikes. "I might; there were a couple I wouldn't mind seeing again. You?"

"There were two or three I'd like to meet up with again. What have I got to lose?"

Chapter 3: Romance with a Hint of Scrutiny

It was almost an entire week before Jodie got the chance to sit and go through her notes from the speed dating event properly. She transcribed them into a word document to make sense of them. Since she just knew their first names, she decided to scan the notes onto the computer to use as part of her report detailing the evening. She didn't care if it made her look nerdy or even a little desperate; it was how her brain worked. Jodie read through it whilst she sat at her desk, munching on a working lunch that consisted of a salad sandwich and a full fat Coke. Before she could change her mind, she copied and pasted the scanned notes into a draft post to complete at home. Louise could cast her eye over the final post before Jodie published it.

Both women were surprised at how much fun they'd had once the event had gotten started. It had been easy to cram a lot of information into the three minutes allotted to each man before the ridiculous, loud bell sounded and he was moved onto the next table. There hadn't been any meetings that caused all background noise to fade while Jodie and a total stranger gazed into each other's souls and decided they needed to look no further. That sort of thing never happened to her, but she was pleased that not all of the men who had attended were mummy's boys. Quite a few of them had been good looking, and also interesting to talk to. These were the ones she was planning to contact again.

Both she and Louise had received messages, but none from anyone they were interested in. Louise had disregarded the messages without even stopping to think about the bigger picture, while

M.B. Feeney

Jodie felt she owed the men some sort of acknowledgement. She sent each of them a short message stating she wasn't interested 'at this time.'

"You're a sap, my dear," Louise had told her when they met up at lunchtime in their favourite sandwich shop. "Do you think giving them a sense of hope is such a good idea?"

"I'm sure they've sent out messages to women other than me." Jodie prayed this was true. She couldn't quite see herself with a guy who got attached after a three-minute meeting and would send out one message to just one person.

~*~

The screen of the laptop was aggravating Jodie's bright green eyes as she read through the speed dating post and the notes she'd typed up after Louise had given her approval.

~*~*~

28 June 2012 - Romance with a Hint of Scrutiny

(Louise chose the title)

The room wasn't just full of geeks and mummy's boys, who were what Louise and I had expected thanks to the stereotypes of the men who attend these events (see my notes taken on the night below). Some of the guys were actually okay.

Before it even started, I was very tempted not to walk into the pub, but Louise was all forceful and made me. I'm glad she did, and I had a lot of fun. I won't bore you with the details of every single guy who spoke to me, that's what my notes are for, but there are two stand-out conversations I'll try to relay as best as I can remember.

Conversation One:

Phil: *"Hi, I'm Phil."* *points to sticker*

Me: *"Hi, I'm Jodie."* *nervous grin*

Phil: *cuts to the chase* *"Is your underwear a matching set?"*

Me: *"What?"* *very confused and expression of slight shock*

"What the hell does that have to do with anything?"

Phil: *"I'm kind of conducting research into women on the pull. It fascinates me, the amount of effort that's put into ensnaring a mate."* *smarmy grin*

Me: *"Make you feel a bit redundant does it? No longer cock of the walk because women have taken the initiative away from the men? Have you even considered the fact that one reason women make an effort could be because it makes THEM feel good, rather than because they are trying to ensnare some unsuspecting, defenceless man?"*

At this point, I was ready to ring the bloody bell myself just so he would piss off away from me before I knocked his shiny veneers down his throat. I was thankful that I didn't need to, as time had already run out. I was in so much shock from Phil's comments that the next fella had to snap his fingers in front of my face to get my attention.

Conversation Two:

Me: *looks at his sticker* *"Hi, John."*

John: *mumbles* *"Hi."*

M: *"So, tell me about yourself . . ."*

J: *"Um . . . I'm thirty, I work in the city . . ."* *takes nervous sip from his bottle of poncy beer*

M: *"That's . . . err . . . Nice."* *gulp* *"So, you live locally?"*

J: *"Not too far. Me and Mum co-own a house about ten minutes away."* *alarm bells*

M: *"Oh . . . that's great."*

J: *"Er . . . so, what do you do for a living?"*

M: *"I'm a legal secretary."*

tumbleweeds

At that point I'd given up the will to live and knocked back almost a whole large glass of wine. We sat in silence until the bell rang again.

You may have guessed that the two conversations I have posted are the worst of about twenty I had that night. I just wanted to highlight what a lot of women (me included) picture whenever anyone mentions speed dating. Would I go again? Probably, but I have a few messages to follow up on first, and a few of my own to send out.

~*~*~

Jodie didn't publish the post straight away, as she knew that Louise wanted to add her own experiences to it rather than posting separately. Once she closed that tab, she opened the website for Harmonic Speed Dating, the company that had arranged the event, to check whether she had received any messages.

An hour later, she was all caught up. She'd replied in the positive to two messages and had sent out five of her own; that deserved a long soak in a hot bath. There was nothing left to do but wait.

Chapter Four: Bowling for Soup

"Louise, I have a date tomorrow night. What should I wear?" Jodie's voice was calm, belying the nerves she felt. She'd received a response to one of her messages from a man called Paul who, if her notes were correct — and they almost always were — she remembered as tall and broad-shouldered with the most piercing blue eyes she had ever seen, away from a Kemp brother. They'd chatted as if they'd known each other for years, and she remembered being disappointed when the bell rang out, signalling for the men to move on. She hadn't wanted to stop talking to him and had felt a little jealous at the thought of him speaking to another woman.

Paul had remembered liking her — or so he'd said in his message — and had suggested they meet for dinner and drinks. Without hesitation, she'd said yes, and almost a week later, it was panic stations.

"I'll be there in twenty minutes. Don't worry, you'll look luscious as ever."

As Louise hung up, Jodie prayed that her friend wouldn't add this to the blog post later in the week. Up until now, neither of them had made fun of the other, which was strange, but there was always a first time for everything.

Louise arrived armed with a bottle of wine and plenty of enthusiasm. She handed the bottle to Jodie then stalked straight into the bedroom and flung open the wardrobe doors. After pouring out some of the wine, Jodie found her friend perusing her clothes, hand on hips and humming to herself.

"I've already ruled out these three dresses. I think you should wear jeans and a fancy top with those boots." Louise took the glass Jodie offered as she indicated the clothes she was discussing. "Where are you off to, again?"

Jodie groaned. "Bowling . . ." She couldn't believe that someone in his mid-to-late twenties was taking her bowling as if they were teenagers.

"Really? Oh, good God." Louise snorted as she tried not to choke on her wine. She laughed, probably at the idea of Jodie in bowling shoes that had been worn by God knew how many other people. "Jeans and boots, then." She delved into Jodie's tops to find the right one.

Jodie stood there watching her best friend muttering away to herself about, ". . . just the right amount of cleavage."

~*~*~

10 July 2012 - Bowling for Soup

Jodie went on her first date last night with one of the guys from the speed dating gig. He took her . . . bowling. I almost peed my pants when

35

she told me. Seriously, bowling is something teenagers, established couples, or families do on a night out. Not people who are hoping for a second date.

If that wasn't bad enough, Paul arranged for them to meet up at Starbucks (pretentious much?). Could this date scream "awkward teenager" any louder? If it had been suggested to me, I would have told him to stuff it up his . . . well, but it wasn't.

Anyway, off she trotted to meet him, looking gorgeous, and he never showed up. Can you believe it? Paul wasn't late. He just never showed up.

Now, many of us have been stood up before (just check my post from 26 Feb for my own experience), but Jodie never had. Ever. Until now. Unlike most people, who would have gone home and had a glass of something alcoholic and a high-carb microwave meal, Jodie walked into the nearest pub and went on the pull.

Within twenty minutes, she met James: Irish, tall, and VERY good looking (she got a sneaky picture for me when he wasn't looking - almost jet black hair, piercing blue eyes, and did I say tall – I LOVE tall men). Also, he must have had most of the Blarney Stone in his pocket from what she said about his charm, but hey, we all need outrageous flattery once in a while, huh? (By the way, you may be able to tell that I'm a little envious of Jodie right now).

So, they chat away for most of the night. When I say most of the night, I mean they got kicked out of the pub by the poor girl who was trying to clean up and go home. Now, Jodie isn't a big fan of one-night stands as you know, and last night was no different. For all of James's loaded hints, she never gave in (and she wanted to, she told me). Instead, she gave him her number and told him to call her. Which he did THIS LUNCHTIME!!! She's off, out again, on Wednesday. Lucky bitch.

She made me check my messages from the speed dating today . . . I had seven of them. Colour me impressed, and a little bemused. I responded to a couple I had a vague memory of as being pretty decent to talk to and a little easy on the eye. I'm meeting one guy, Steve, for coffee after work

37

tomorrow. Will let you all know how that goes.

~*~*~

Jodie read Louise's post, giggling while she ate her dinner. She loved her friend's no-nonsense style. Although she never minced her words or held back, it was never Louise's intent to hurt with her honesty, either, and that shone through in all the blog posts she'd written.

Jodie had been just as surprised at meeting James Branson as Louise had been. When she'd been stood up by Paul, she had gone into the pub — not on the pull as Louise had made out, but to save a little face before going back home for a night in front of the telly. She decided to hit the big stuff and had ordered a double vodka and orange when James had bumped her whilst playing a game of pool. Since he hadn't been playing very well, he was happy to throw the game and flirt instead.

When the poor girl behind the bar had to beg them to leave so she could go home, James had walked her to the nearest taxi rank, hinting about "coffee."

As much as they had hit it off, she didn't do first-date sex. She hadn't told him that; she'd just decided to play a little hard to get. She did give him her number, though, and a goodnight kiss — or three — before hopping into a cab, leaving him wanting more.

Chapter Five: Take a Chance

"Jodie and James, eh? You sound like a dodgy celeb couple." Louise snickered while they sat in the pub, waiting for their lunch to arrive.

"Oh, shut up. We do not." Jodie got a case of the warm fuzzies at the mention of James's name but had managed to hide the fact from her friend. They'd met up once more, and he seemed to understand her desire to take things slowly. She'd never said so aloud, but even so, he wasn't pressuring her into meeting all the time or into taking things further.

"Oh, 'we' already?" Louise couldn't help but tease. "Next you'll be too busy buying curtains for your new place with him to spend time with me. I'll be the old crone at your wedding . . ." She couldn't carry on speaking through her laughter.

"Piss off, you idiot. We've been in each other's company less than a handful of times. I wouldn't start booking wedding venues."

"Not just yet . . ."

Jodie slapped her friend's arm none too gently to shut her up when their food arrived.

"Enough about me. How did the meeting with Steve Alden go?" A grin spread across Louise's face, which Jodie knew meant just one thing. "Already?" She was incredulous.

"What? You know how it goes when a man and a woman meet up, are attracted to each other . . ."

"But you just met for coffee."

"Coffee soon became dinner and drinks." Louise took a sip of her wine to wash down some of her food.

"So, are you seeing him again?"

"I doubt it."

41

Typical Louise. Sleeps with a guy on the first date, and then she loses interest. Jodie had always thought she liked the chase more than anything.

"What's wrong with this one?"

"There's nothing 'wrong' with him . . ." Jodie waited for the inevitable "but" that she knew would follow. "But he just seems a little clingy."

"How can you tell he's clingy? You spent one night with him."

"Er. . ." Louise started to giggle. "Steve cried when I got dressed to leave after we'd finished. He said that women never stay over."

"Why didn't you just stay the night? I know you; you like snuggles and wake up sex."

"His flat was mingin'. It was filthy."

Jodie could almost see Louise's skin crawling from the memory.

"It's not funny. There were dirty plates and cups all over the place, and I think he was trying to cultivate penicillin in some of them. It was horrid, and the smell? Jesus, I think the stench in the air took off a layer of skin when I first walked in."

Jodie couldn't stop laughing at the mental images. Even though Louise was the scattiest person Jodie had ever met, she was the poster child for OCD when it came to her flat.

"What excuse did you use when you left?"

"I didn't. I was so disgusted, I couldn't think straight and just blurted out the truth, then ran like a bat out of hell." That intensified Jodie's laughter even more. "It's not funny, Jode. My skin was crawling. I had to have a shower as soon as I got in. It's such a shame, 'cause he was lovely, and he knew what he was doing between th- oh, God. The sheets." A horrified look crossed her face as she scratched at her bare arm.

"Well . . . that'll teach you not to be such a trollop."

Louise just rolled her eyes and ignored her friend, just as she did every time Jodie teased her.

"So, if he contacts you, you won't be seeing him again, then?"

"I don't know. I might do; I'll just make sure I never go back to his place. But as I told him the truth, I doubt he'd be interested in meeting up again, do you?" Jodie knew Louise would be quietly hoping Steve would contact her again, since he was just her type. He was very tall and had dark hair, dark eyes, and an olive complexion. Lou wouldn't be able to resist.

~*~*~

18 July 2012 - Take a Chance. . .

So — I saw James again, but more about that in a while. First, I need to tell you about the second meeting between Lou and Steve. That's the first time I've known her to meet up with someone after she's decided not to see them again. Under normal circumstances, when Louise decides she won't see someone again, she sticks to it. He must have been pretty special in bed if she not only took his call, but also agreed to meet for a drink. This time, she'd learnt from her mistakes and took him to her place. In fact, they spent most of the weekend holed up in her cosy little flat. I didn't hear from her for almost two days, which is unheard of.

When I did hear from Louise, she was acting like a giddy sixteen-year-old. It was apparent that Steve had taken notice of what she'd said. He was now in the process of sorting his flat out, but he also wants to cook dinner for her to say "thank you" one night next week. She's going to inspect his handiwork the day before, and if it meets her standards, she is going to suggest that he invite me and James to join them. This scares me somewhat.

James . . . the marvellous James took me for a wonderful dinner at this tiny little steak house that I never knew existed. The food was amazing, the atmosphere was perfect, and we got on well. He told about life growing up just outside Cork, while I told him about never having lived anywhere but

45

London. We talked about our Uni days and careers. James found my being a legal secretary fascinating — I don't know why, since he works in aviation. He works for Boeing doing something . . . important. I can't remember what it is he does. It all sounded a bit scary. I mean, one little mistake . . .

shudder

Anyway, James was fantastic, the food was amazing, but there seemed to be no

. . . spark this time. I just didn't feel very comfortable, and I don't know why. I was surprised, considering that we'd gotten on fine at our last two meetings and we'd been texting or emailing pretty much all the time. It just felt forced — to me, at least. James didn't seem to notice that there was anything wrong, or if he did, he kept it to himself and put on a good show.

Things seemed to get a little more relaxed once we'd finished eating and decided to take a walk along the embankment. Maybe it made a difference being out in the open air and not surrounded by lots of other couples who seemed much more at ease with each other. As we began to walk to the tube station, I started to consider inviting James to the flat to see where things went. Just as I opened my mouth to mention it, his phone rang, and he had to dash off because of some kind of emergency at work. So he left me a little breathless and a lot turned on from his goodbye kiss. Git. Looking back, I should have sent a text to him to read when he finished work.

Next time, I will. I promise.

~*~*~

Chapter Six: Back in the Game

Jodie spent the weekend taking a break from the computer and catching up with some reading. She had a pile of books beside her bed that she'd been meaning to make a dent in for a while. Although she didn't read as often as she would have liked anymore, when a book hooked her from the get-go, she would devour it in a matter of hours.

With her phone switched to silent — she never could turn it off altogether — and her iPod on shuffle with the volume on low, she spent the entire weekend seated in the squashy armchair by the front room window in her pyjamas, doing nothing other than reading. The only time she got up was to either go to the bathroom or to make a fresh cup of tea or a round of toast.

It had been so long since she had done something she saw as decadent that she felt a little guilty when Louise let herself into the flat looking for her.

"Why haven't you been answering your phone?" Louise's voice sounded a little frantic as she stared at Jodie. "And why are you still in your pyjamas?"

Jodie watched her friend flop onto the sofa. "I decided to have a weekend just for me. Recharge the batteries, so to speak. Is that a crime?"

"I guess not, but why haven't you answered the phone?"

Jodie picked up her phone to see that she had eight missed calls in the last hour and numerous messages. "I had the phone on silent so I wouldn't be disturbed."

Louise looked a little uncomfortable. "Sorry." She stood up, making Jodie think she was going to leave. "Tea?"

Or not . . . "Sure."

Louise didn't hear the sigh her friend expelled as Jodie closed her book and stood up to stretch out her muscles. "I'm just going to grab a quick shower." Her weekend of luxury was at an end.

~*~*~

25 July 2012 – Back in the Game

Having a weekend of doing nothing is a luxury I could get used to having. Not once did I turn on the computer to check my messages. I switched my phone to silent and took it off vibrate and just read (which got me in trouble with Lou). I even managed to avoid mushy chick lit books, too; I didn't think reading those would have helped much, considering stuff like that never happens to me and falls under the realm of unrealistic in my experience.

When I got into work on Monday, I checked all my emails and speed dating messages. I was lucky that all the partners were out of the office, because I was going to be very busy sifting and responding.

When Lou turned up at my flat, she told me all about the message she'd received in her blog email (if you need either of us, look in contacts) from a guy who said he'd been reading the blog for a while now and that he wanted to take her out for dinner. He'd attached pictures of himself and had given her a synopsis of his entire life story. She wasn't sure what to do. I couldn't tell her what to decide, so — here's the point of today's post.

We're putting Lou's decision to the public vote. You have twenty-four hours in which to choose whether she goes out with him. You will not be given any information about him until after the poll has ended. Click here to vote."

~*~*~

Jodie understood Louise's hesitation. Neither of them had ever been contacted via the blog email like that. Connor seemed like a nice guy, if the information he'd sent was to be believed, and he looked a bit dishy in the picture, if it was a real photo of him. It wasn't the thought of him having lied or even stretched the truth about himself to get a date, which was possible — they'd both been in that position. It was the fact that he'd read the blog that freaked Louise out most of all. He already knew all about her and had fed her information based on what he'd read.

"Lou, in all honesty, it's a sodding miracle that he's read the blog and still hasn't run a mile knowing how bloody high-maintenance you are."

"Ha ha, very funny."

Jodie stuck out her tongue.

"I don't know why I'm so freaked out by knowing he knows all about me. It's not like I say anything on there I would never say to someone's face."

That was true beyond a doubt.

"Look, you've gone on a date with a guy knowing less, in all honesty. What's the harm?"

"I guess. We've put it to the readers, so just wait and see what they say."

Jodie grinned. She'd never seen her friend so indecisive about a guy before.

"Enough about me. How's the wonderful James?" Louise laughed at the blush caused by the mention of the Irishman's name.

"He's . . . wonderful."

"Pathetic answer. Have you heard from him since you didn't invite him over for 'coffee'?"

"Yeah, he's over in Dublin for some meetings. We're going out next Saturday when he gets back."

"Ooh. How many dates is that now? Three? Four?"

"Four . . . I think. I'm not keeping count." She wasn't. For the first time in a long time, Jodie was just taking each date as it happened. It felt good not to stress. She would be lying if she didn't admit to hoping it would lead to something more, but she was happy to just spend time with James.

"Yeah, right. Since when?"

"Since meeting him wasn't planned. It's been so long since I've met someone without planning pretty much every aspect. Meeting James was a fluke, so there's little to no expectation tacked onto every date."

Louise considered what Jodie said. "That makes sense. It's like when you're a teenager: you met guys everywhere and never expected every single one of them to be the one and just had fun."

"Exactly." Jodie grinned. "So where's he taking you?"

"I have no idea. He said to dress down." Louise shuddered. No good ever came of a date that didn't include heels. Or so she believed.

Chapter Seven: Next Time, Call a Decorator

Jodie was surprised to find that she missed James. They'd quickly become friends and were in almost-constant contact. This allowed them to get to know each other, but she didn't want to get her hopes up about him. Too many times she'd done just that, and things hadn't worked out, causing inevitable heartache to follow. Too many times she'd had to pick herself up and dust herself down to start over with Louise's help. She didn't want to go through that again.

The two friends had been there for each other since their early teens, having met in Secondary School. They were like chalk and cheese, but they'd managed to surprise everyone by being the perfect buffer for each other. Louise was the confident, outgoing, pretty brunette who seemed to attract all the attention from the boys, whilst Jodie was a quiet redhead. She was grateful that Louise always made her feel that she was capable of anything and supported any choices she made. Jodie tried to do the same for Louise, even after being honest with her when she didn't agree with them. That was the makings of a good friendship . . . wasn't it?

For the next twenty years, they met up or spoke every day. When they went away to university, they managed to meet up at least twice a month, either in Nottingham, where Louise studied English Literature, or in Manchester, where Jodie studied History. Neither of them judged the other on mistakes made under the influence of student nights or the fact that neither was using her degree. To be honest, Jodie couldn't imagine not having Louise in her life, and any men they met had to accept them as a package deal.

~*~*~

5 August 2012- Next Time, Call a Decorator

James arrived on my doorstep on Friday with flowers and a bottle of Irish whiskey, fresh from his return to London. Reminding me that I was to dress down for our day out on Saturday, he refused my invitation inside for a drink (damn him). Apparently, it would be helpful for me to conserve energy. Yeah, that snippet of information didn't help me to relax.

He turned up to collect me at 8a.m., causing me to almost pass out. I'd only just clambered out of the shower and hadn't even had a cup of tea. It was lucky that he'd shown up early in case he needed to wake me up, and I still had an hour before we had to leave.

Dressing down to me means huge jogging bottoms, an out-of-shape men's T-shirt, and big fluffy socks, but I knew that wouldn't do. I managed to find an old pair of combat trousers, which, when teamed with a vest top and my boots, James announced were perfect before he handed me a travel mug of tea and led me out to his car.

He didn't blindfold me or anything ridiculous like that, but he wouldn't answer any of my questions. It was only when we'd arrived that I cottoned on. Paintballing! It was something I'd always said I wanted to try, but I knew I'd never have the bottle to sign up for it. A bit like Zumba.

It was bloody brilliant — and painful. I never expected that at all, even after watching people do it on the telly. They never quite tell you HOW MUCH it hurts, even with the breastplate women are given for extra protection. But it was all so worth it.

Remember that scene in "10 Things I Hate About You," where Heath takes whatsername paintballing and they kiss? Well, it was nothing like that . . . there was more adrenaline, masks, and guns. We must have played for about three hours straight until my legs were like jelly and my body was aching. When I told James how much I hurt, he told me that he'd run me a hot bath when we got back to mine. And he did. It was wonderful. The massage that followed was even better.

We both woke up this morning covered in bruises.

~*~*~

"He stayed the fucking night?" Louise's voice was so shrill down the phone, it caused Jodie to wince and hold the phone away from her ear.

"He did." She couldn't wipe the grin off her face at the memories of James kissing, teasing, and caressing her all night.

"So why am I hearing about it now via a bloody blog post?"

"Because you've had your phone switched off all day." Jodie could imagine why that was. "It's not what you think. Me and Steve are no more."

"Oh? Why's that? I thought you were getting on well." Jodie was a little shocked. She had thought that Louise was willing to give the relationship with Steve a go.

59

"We were. He turned up at mine a little worse for wear and proceeded to call me a cock tease, and to add insult to injury, he called me a slag." Jodie's gasp of outrage spurred Louise on with her story. "Yeah, so after I slapped him, he told me not to bother contacting him again."

"So, what brought all this on, then?"

Jodie hooked the phone between her shoulder and her ear as she moved around the kitchen making a cup of tea, wincing from the delicious ache in her body.

"He didn't appreciate that I was considering going on a date with someone I didn't know. Apparently, putting my decision to the public vote like that made me look desperate."

"Oh, really? And you knew him so well when you met up with him. Prick."

"Indeed. So, I've decided I'm not pulling out of meeting up with Connor."

"I didn't know you were considering it."

"Of course I was. It's one thing to be set up on a blind date by Theresa, but our readers want to see us find the right guys for us, so this is a different kettle of fish altogether."

She had a point.

"Have you emailed him yet?"

"Not yet. I was hoping you'd help."

"Wuss." Jodie grinned.

"Of course. I'll be over in half an hour if that's okay."

"When is it ever not?" They ended their call.

While she put a bottle of wine into the fridge to chill, Jodie wondered if Connor was quite sure what he was letting himself in for by asking Louise for a date.

Chapter Eight: Is 'The Chase' Worth It?

Jodie was like a woman possessed. She couldn't get enough of James whenever they were in each other's company. It was like she had regressed to a horny sixteen-year-old who needed to get as much as she could before curfew. James didn't seem to complain much as he made the most of being desired by a woman, and he returned Jodie's affections — often. They both knew that the newness would wear off; it always did as the honeymoon period began to wane.

Having been with James for over six weeks caused a bit of a slump in Jodie's posts on the blog. After all, how often could she post about a wonderful date followed by wonderful sex with the same man? Louise, on the other hand, was still searching. As envious asshe was of Jodie having found a good guy, she was over the moon for her friend. Jodie had never believed that she was desirable and that men were attracted to her. Maybe James could be the one to get her to see herself in a new light.

If Louise was honest with herself, Steve flipping out on her had hurt more than she let on to anyone. She was getting bored of always being on the lookout for the next date, and the thrill of the chase was losing its appeal. She knew she shouldn't allow men to see her as an easy lay, but she liked sex and wasn't afraid to enjoy it as often as possible, but even that was getting stale. She craved more.

Louise had started to think that she could have that more with Steve, especially after he'd cleared up the utter dump his flat had been. He was a decent guy, treated her well, and was good in bed. So why did she have to go and balls it up with the email? Oh yeah, 'cause that's what she did.

~*~

Jodie watched as Louise got herself ready for her date with David, whom she'd met through Connor the email guy when they'd realised they were better off being good friends. Her friend seemed to be going through the motions without any true enthusiasm.

"You okay, Lou?"

"Of course. Just a little nervous." She didn't look nervous; she looked disinterested, which was new. Louise always got excited about a first date, but this time . . . it was almost like she couldn't be bothered and didn't want to be going.

"You don't seem your usual chipper self this evening." Jodie handed over the shoes she had been asked to pull out of the wardrobe. "Are you sure nothing's wrong?"

"I'm fine. Bloody hell, Jode; give me a break, will you?" Louise had never snapped at Jodie like that. Jodie kept her cool as she gathered her bag and jacket to prevent any arguments starting.

"Fine. Call me when you get over yourself and have stopped chucking your toys out the pram." Without looking back, Jodie let herself out of the flat and started on the short walk home.

~*~*~

9 September 2012- Is 'The Chase' Worth It?

Last night, I found I was asking myself what the point was to all the games we play when we're dating. I mean, are all the fuss and bother worth a fumble and a possible second date that will no doubt be just as awkward as the first — maybe even more so, as memories of what the person sitting opposite you looks like naked run through your head?

David, bless him, was lovely. Too much so, if I'm honest. I didn't think blokes like that existed anymore, you know the kind: they hold doors open and pull out your chair. His mother

65

should be very proud. But is it enough to have flawless manners all the time? Now and then, he must have the need to get down and dirty, even if just for one night.

If he does, it wasn't with me, that was for sure. No, we had a nice dinner, followed by a nice chat over coffee. Then, a nice stroll (I NEVER stroll) as he walked me home. I invited him in for coffee, but he refused. He had to be up early this morning to do his volunteer work. Really? Am I being too cynical? A quick peck on the cheek, a half-hearted promise to be in touch, and I'm home alone with a cup of tea.

I couldn't even phone Jodie to moan 'cause I pissed her off by being a grumpy bitch. (We've sorted it now, but last night I knew to leave well enough alone. When Jodie's pissed off, it's best to let her stew for at least twelve hours. After that she's ready to talk things over, but before . . . she's apt to bite your head off.)

I am doubtful I'll see David again. He was nice, but . . . yeah, nice. I need more than nice; I need someone who's not going to put up with my crappy mood swings; someone who challenges me. We need intellectual as well as physical compatibility. I want what Jodie and James (I can't type that without sniggering and hearing a superhero theme tune in my head) seem to have.

~*~*~

Louise read the post over to check for any spelling and grammar errors before she posted it. She couldn't remember the last time she'd felt so down about the state of her love life. "State" was the right word. Ever since Connor had emailed her to ask her out, things had gone downhill fast.

A couple of times, she'd considered calling Steve or even showing up at his door, but she was too scared by the possibility that he'd found someone better. It was the typical case of not knowing what you've got until it's gone. Looking back, she realised that she'd actually had Steve. Why else would he have gotten drunk and upset at the thought of her dating Connor? Or was she reading too much into the whole thing? She'd done that before and ended up looking like a complete fool.

"I've become a chick flick cliché at last," she mumbled to herself as she pressed publish and poured herself a glass of wine. "All I need now is to bump into 'the one that got away' and his gorgeous and nubile new wife or fiancée to make things extra crappy."

Chapter Nine: Do My High Street Bargains Offend You?

Jodie sat looking at James as he told her about his recent work trip to New York. She thought back to the date when she'd thought there'd been no spark between them. That was as far from the situation now as possible; the spark was so strong, it was almost visible. James grinned at her when he caught her watching his hands, knowing exactly where they'd been just over an hour before they'd arrived at the restaurant.

"See something you like?" he teased her without warning, catching her off guard.

"Nope, nothing." She played nonchalant as she picked at her food. "Nothing at all." It was obvious that he didn't believe her.

"I'd love nothing more than to take you back to mine and worship you all night; it's unfortunate that our guests have just arrived." He turned away, a large smile plastered to his face.

~*~*~

20 September 2012- Do My High Street Bargains Offend You?

It's taken me two days to write this post to prevent its being an entire post of my effing and blinding, thus offending every single reader we have. I have been pissed off since Friday evening and with good reason . . . or so I believe.

James had been in New York for a few days for work, so I was a little excited at the thought of seeing him again. In fact, I showed him just how excited I was as soon as he walked into my flat, even though we were supposed to be getting ready to go out with his friends. Eventually, we were composed enough to leave.

James's friends were a decent bunch for the most part. The guys all flirted in a merciless, yet harmless, way with me in an effort to try and wind him up. Not once did he bite, which led me to believe it wasn't something new, but he did lay his arm across the back of my chair and stroke the back of my neck. This did not go unnoticed, and he endured a fair bit of piss-taking for it. He didn't care.

A few of the guys had brought along their girlfriends or wives, who all welcomed me into their circle without question. We chatted about Sunday morning football matches (they watched from the warmth of a car with a thermos of coffee in the winter), nights out together, and one ill-fated group holiday to a caravan park in Wales.

I was enjoying myself and getting a little drunk, when Amy turned up. She was gorgeous: statuesque, with beautiful, deep-chestnut hair, and the figure of a pin-up. I felt like a spotty teenager when she walked into the room. The girls I was talking to all gave her welcoming smiles and hugged her, but I could see that their expressions were tense and the embraces not as warm as they appeared. It was obvious to me that they either didn't like her or didn't trust her. I watched them watching Amy as she greeted all the guys with enthusiastic

71

hugs and air kisses, which were
returned half-heartedly. It was
obvious that she was single, yet she
was still part of the group. Maybe one
of them was an ex, or perhaps a family
member? Why else would she be there?

James must have sensed I was uneasy,
because he came over to me and joined
in my conversation with the other
girls. He chatted with us all, making
us laugh, and treated each of the
ladies to the same outrageous flirting
I had endured upon my arrival. Amy
joined us once she'd bought herself a
drink, at once honing in on me.

All seemed to be going okay until she
asked about my outfit. You should have
seen the sneer when I told her that my
jeans, top, and boots had all come
from my favourite High Street shop. I
don't think her lip could have curled
back any more. I mean, her designer
jeans cost about four times as mine
and didn't look THAT different.
Denim's denim, at the end of the day.
There may also have been a snotty
comment about looking cheap and
getting what you paid for, but I may
have imagined that.

From what I gathered, she doesn't do much for a living and hangs around with the team all the time. After James re-joined the guys, Amy went to "powder her nose," and Stacey, one of the wives, told me that she literally had meant powder. None of the women liked Amy, since she'd been caught more than once trying it on with unavailable players. I couldn't understand why she hadn't been told to take a running jump, and I said as much to Stacey.

"Her dad owns the team," she explained.

Say no more.

~*~*~

"So, let me get everything straight in my mind. Her dad owns the team, pays for the kit and facilities, and all that jazz?" Louise asked, her voice revealing her anger at Amy's behaviour.

Jodie nodded, knowing a rant was coming.

"So, what the fuck gives her the right to try it on with married and taken fellas? I mean, seriously

— I would have slapped her silly if she'd done that to me. Why has no one told her to piss off and to leave the team alone?"

"She threatens to get Daddy to pull the funding. None of the blokes have been stupid enough to take her up on any of her offers, but it doesn't stop her trying. She doesn't even want a relationship with any of them — just a fling before she finds some rich fat cat to keep her in the lifestyle she has been accustomed to."

"Well, she needs to get accustomed to a punch in the face off the wives and girlfriends . . ." Louise trailed off, sniggering to herself.

"What's so funny?" Jodie asked, confused.

"You're a WAG." Lou's sniggering turned into full-blown hysterical laughter.

Jodie was horrified. "Oh, good God! No, no — it doesn't count if they're only a Sunday League team."

"It's a football team, however amateur they are. You know what this means now, don't you?" Louise seemed to be enjoying herself a little too much.

"No . . ."

"Three layers of fake tan, three inch acrylic nails, and shitty hair extensions." Louise couldn't carry on and fell about laughing so much she couldn't breathe.

"You bitch. You scared me!" Jodie hated it when Louise teased her.

"Sorry, but it was worth it just to see the look of horror on your face."

"Remind me to never invite you to a team 'do then."

"Any single players?" Louise sat up straight, focussed on the thought of new prospective dates.

"You'll never know, now will you?" Jodie cackled at the pout on her friend's face.

"Who's the bitch now?"

That just set Jodie's laughter off again until she fell out of her chair for real.

Chapter Ten: To Quote Cher: 'If I Could Turn Back Time'

Louise checked the messages on her phone and found a couple more from David. She deleted them without responding, still unsure how to turn him down without hurting his feelings. There was absolutely nothing wrong with him. He was kind and courteous, and her mother would love him. He just wasn't Steve. Usually, she would have been happy to go out with him again and again, but a nice guy just wasn't enough anymore. That's what scared her. Once she'd been dumped, she never lingered, and had always been able to get over it and move on, whether there was a new man in the picture or not.

Louise had tried to work out how to contact Steve again without him telling her to get lost. She wanted to explain, but she wasn't quite sure if she could get him to listen and to change his mind about her. Jodie had noticed that Louise's enthusiasm for dating anyone, not just David, had all but disappeared and had asked what was going on. Louise hadn't known what to say, so she said nothing. Jodie didn't push; she knew that Louise would tell her when she was ready.

~*~*~

30 September 2012 – To Quote Cher: 'If I Could Turn Back Time'

We all have dating regrets. It's usual for them to involve someone we went out with (set up as a blind date, more often than not) whom we wouldn't have looked at twice under any other circumstances. These are often the ones who message us non-stop about going out again.

Every now and then, a nice guy shows up on the radar and is such a change that we get caught up in being treated like a princess. This is almost always the end of the dating, since the nice guy is the one who becomes the

78

partner, the husband, and sometimes even the father. So why can't I settle for that? And why can't I find a gentle way to let him down?

I think it was Joni Mitchell who sang: "You don't know what you got 'til it's gone," (although I have to admit, I prefer the Counting Crows version just because his voice is gorgeous). I'd never gotten it, but I do now. I'm just wondering if there's any way to get it back once I get the nerve to set everything straight.

Jesus Christ, I sound so maudlin. I think the problem is that too many people, most often women, put so much emphasis on who they are in a relationship with or dwell too much if they aren't in one, which can cause them to lose sight of what is important in life. Why should it matter if we are single at twenty-four or not? Then again, that's easy for me to say, but I am also the first one to think I am undesirable if I'm single. Jodie does it too; we're designed to think that way.

Sex sells. We all know that; it's all around us, TV, film, advertising . . . being a single woman has never been acceptable in our society,in particular if it goes on for too long. It's fine for men to be 'eternal bachelors' and to stick to casual dating, but if women do the same? They are branded "spinsters" or "slappers." I'm not getting into the whole men vs. women debate now, but the old game of double standards is still very much in motion and always will be. That's an unfortunate fact of life.

I guess the point behind this post (somewhere; I ramble) is that we need to consider our decisions when it comes to not just who we settle down with, but also who we spend our time with before then. For me, in particular, I've come to realise that I also need to stop taking people at face value and give myself a bit of time to get to know someone. It's not just about being physical; that bond is easy to forget. It's also about creating an emotional bond. I've come to the conclusion that friends make the best lovers.

~*~*~

Jodie wanted to hug Louise after reading the latest post, but her friend was out of the city visiting her parents, who had retired to Devon. She suspected Louise had gone down to escape making a final choice between David and Connor. Jodie still didn't know the whole story, but she knew her friend well enough to read between the lines of her posts and to hear the words Louise wasn't saying during their conversations.

She wanted to help Louise, but she knew that if she tried to get involved, she could make things worse. Jodie didn't want to do that. Louise had so much love to give; she just needed to find the right person.

"What's wrong, honey?" James emerged from the bathroom wrapped in her huge terry towelling gown, rubbing his damp hair with a towel.

"Nothing, really. I just wish I could help Lou. I don't think she realises how much sadness comes pouring out of her posts on the blog."

He stood behind her and read the post over her shoulder. "Has she talked about this with you?" he asked a few minutes later.

"No, and I wish she would. It's so obvious that she's regretting the decision to accept the initial date with Connor." Jodie thought back to the date that had never been documented on the blog since Louise had refused to make either of them look foolish. "And what makes it worse is that as soon as they met, it was obvious they wouldn't ever be more than good friends who met for a coffee now and then. They were both fine with that, but if she had never considered going on that date, she might well still be with Steve."

"Which one was Steve?" James couldn't keep up.

"Messy flat." He nodded to indicate he remembered.

"I think in the short time they could have been considered a couple, Louise caught a glimpse of what could be, and now she regrets not seeing where it was destined to lead them."

"Is it so hard for her to just contact him and talk it through?"

"I don't think it's that simple. It's obvious that she blames herself for throwing away the opportunity with him and doesn't quite know how to claw her way back into his life."

James kissed the top of her head as he stood. "She needs to just be honest with him."

Jodie watched him go into her bedroom to get dressed. How had she struck it so lucky meeting him? She grinned to herself like a fool as she waited for him to get ready so they could venture together into the hell that was meeting her parents for dinner.

Chapter Eleven: Meet the Parents

~*~*~

14 October 2012 – Meet the Parents

There's one milestone out of the way. Last week, I received a phone call from my mum. Don't get me wrong; I love my parents to bits, but Mum can be a little overbearing at times. I know it's just because she wants the best for me and for me to be happy. She's the same with my sister Hannah, but sometimes she can be a bit full-on without meaning to be. Anyway, she was insisting that she and Dad treat me to a nice dinner at the Italian by their house, and of course, "you need to bring that young man you've been spending so much time with." Like I didn't expect that.

James was all for it, of course. He said he couldn't wait to meet them (I think he gushed about thanking them for having me or some such nonsense, but I didn't pay much attention to that. He knows that stuff embarrasses me), and that it was a shame that Hannah wasn't going to be there as well. Thank Christ she's tramping around South America for her gap year. I couldn't have coped with her and Mum ganging up on me about James and his "prospects."

I don't think it could have gone better even if I'd planned it. James charmed my mother. It was "Mrs Fletcher" this and "Mrs Fletcher" that the whole night. Dad just liked the fact that James designed planes. Poor Dad had wanted to be in the Air Force but couldn't because he's colour blind. He's still fascinated by anything to do with aviation, though, and he will jump at the chance to blather on about it with a willing partner.

Looking back, I don't know why I was worried about James meeting my parents at all. He is charming, articulate, and makes me happy. What more could my parents want? Although my mother is now hinting about grandchildren, and not very subtly, either. As usual, I've been ignoring her and just enjoying having someone who likes spending time with me and doesn't care that I look like the Wild Woman of Wonga first thing in the morning.

I just wish Lou was experiencing the same. Even though she hasn't told me the whole story about what's bugging her, I know she deserves to be happy. I know settling down isn't the answer to everyone's happiness, but Lou should have the opportunity to spend time with a guy who wants to be with her. It doesn't need to be the love affair of the century; it just needs to be mutual.

~*~*~

"So, has James asked your dad for permission to propose, then?" Louise looked tanned after her week in Devon.

"Propose?" Jodie spluttered. "After two months? Please."

"It's not completely unheard of."

"Look, we're not getting engaged. We're just taking each day as it comes."

"Okay. What about moving in together?"

"Bloody hell, Lou. Why are you so intent on me and James being serious all of a sudden?" Jodie smiled so that Louise knew she wasn't having a go.

"I don't know. You're just both . . . I don't know." Louise couldn't quite verbalise what she was trying to say. "It's like you said in your post. What you and James have is mutual." She shook her head as if to reassemble her thoughts.

"I know what you mean," Jodie helped. "Have you told David that you won't be seeing him again yet?"

"Yeah, I called him at lunchtime."

"How did he take it?"

"He was fine. I explained that under different circumstances, I think it would have worked."

"Different to what?" Jodie was determined to get the truth out of Louise once and for all.

Her friend took a deep breath. "Different as in if I weren't pining after Steve like a horny teenager."

"Is that all it is? Horniness?" Jodie didn't believe that was all it was. "I think there's more to it than missing the sex." She was surprised to find Louise close to tears. "Oh, honey. It's not that bad."

"Isn't it? I was so close to maybe finding . . . mutual, and I threw it away over an email and a fucking public blog vote." Louise took a few more deep breaths to hold back the tears that were threatening to spill. "I think I was too busy thinking about the next blog post and a new way of meeting someone that I'd forgotten what I was looking for in the first place." This time, she didn't even bother fighting the tears, just letting them fall.

"Hey, stop beating yourself up. You got a little carried away. We've all been there. The main thing is not to dwell on where you think you went wrong, but how you're going to make it right." Jodie handed Louise a wad of tissue to wipe her eyes and to blow her nose.

"Well?"

"Well, what?"

"Well . . . How are you going to get back in contact with Steve to find out if he's the "mutual" for you?"

"I have no idea. I can't just text him; he'd just ignore it. And I doubt he'd answer a call from me."

"It's unfortunate, but I think you might be right." Jodie poured them both a fresh glass of wine. "Can you remember his address?" The look on Louise's face answered that question. "Well, write it down for me. I'm taking the day off tomorrow."

"You can't go round there. What if he's met someone else?"

"I can, and I will. Even if he's got someone else, he needs to know. I know for a fact that you won't do it, so I'm going." Jodie took the piece of paper from her friend and tucked it into her bag. "I won't make you look like a fool, but I will tell him you regret certain choices. Then, I'll leave the ball in his court. What could go wrong?"

"Did you really ask that? What a way to put a jinx on the entire thing!" Louise grumbled as she knocked back half a glass of wine.

"Don't be ridiculous. Everything will be fine. I'll make sure of it." There was no point in arguing. Jodie was stubborn to the point of ignorance sometimes.

"Wonderful." Louise cradled her head in her hands.

M.B. Feeney

Chapter Twelve: Return of the Mack

Jodie checked the address against the one Louise had given her. It was the right place; she just needed to pluck up the courage to go and knock on his door. She hadn't quite thought through a plan of action before blurting it out to Louise the previous evening, but she would have said anything to stop seeing her friend so upset.

While she gathered her bag and phone, psyching herself up to get out of the car, she saw him leave the flat, turn, and walk in the opposite direction.

"Fabulous. Do I sit and hang around like a stalker, or do I get out and follow him like a stalker?" she grumbled to herself. Lucky for her, in the rear view mirror she saw him enter the newsagent's on the corner. A few minutes later, her patience was rewarded with him coming out and walking back in her direction. Grinning, she watched him let himself back into his flat.

~*~*~

15 October 2012 - Return of the Mack

(Well, not really. I just had that song on my iPod.)

I know there was a post yesterday, but I wanted to tell you about my adventure today. So, it was mission 'get Steve to talk to Louise' day. I took a day off that I was owed from work and drove over to Steve's place to try and talk to him.

You will be pleased to know, as was Lou when I told her, that there is no new woman. I'm not just going off a hunch; I straight-up asked him. (And yes, his flat is still clean.)

Steve was a little surprised to see me, but he'd been reading the blog and was close to contacting Louise himself. That shocked me a little. I thought he hated her, but he soon set me straight. Even though he'd felt betrayed, he admitted to missing her.

He explained that although they weren't in an official committed relationship, the fact that she'd been considering other dates had still hurt him. The entire situation had caused him to have many an internal argument about whether he had the right to feel that way and if he should get in contact with her to try and straighten things out. He likened it to the Ross/Rachel 'we were on a break' storyline in Friends. Steve felt like Rachel, oddly enough.

Then it was my turn. I told him all about my conversation with Lou last night. From his reaction, he hadn't considered it the way Lou did, and I know she hadn't thought about things from his perspective. I swear, I should have done this ages ago. They deserve to have their heads banged together. Anyway, I left him to think about what I had said. I'd been at Lou's for about forty-five minutes when he rang her, asking if they could meet up. (Guess where they are now.)

I believe my work here is done. I'm just unsure what is going to happen with the blog now.

~*~*~

Jodie couldn't wipe the smug smile off her face as she watched James cook for them. She also couldn't stop looking at her phone every five minutes to check for messages from Louise.

"Put that phone away before I confiscate it, Cupid."

She jumped at the sound of James's voice. "But . . ."

He crossed the room and took the phone out of her hand, switching it off and sliding it into his pocket. "No buts. Let them get on with it. Louise will call you tomorrow, of that I have no doubt." He grinned and kissed her pouty lips.

"I hate you." Jodie grinned.

"No you don't."

No, she didn't. In fact she . . . no, she wasn't going to think about it. It was far too soon.

Instead, she stuck her tongue out before sipping at the red wine in front of her, but it didn't help. Those three little words were dancing on the tip of her tongue, teasing her. Jodie and James had known each other for a couple of months, which was nowhere near long enough to start entertaining those kinds of thoughts. She needed her phone so she could message Louise, but as she'd been cut off and Louise was with Steve, there was no chance of her friend helping her through the anxiety that was starting to grip her.

"Are you okay?" James asked as he placed the food in front of her.

"I'm fine. Just a little nervous for Lou."

He chuckled as he began to eat, not noticing how strained her smile was and that she was just pushing her food around her plate rather than eating it. She ate a few mouthfuls, but everything tasted like cardboard, so she gave up and pushed the plate away from her.

"Are you sure nothing's wrong?" James put his own cutlery down and took her hands in his, worry etched across every inch of his face.

"I think I'm getting a migraine. I'm going to jump in a cab and go home to lie down. I'm sorry. I've ruined dinner after you spent so much time cooking."

"You've ruined nothing. Let me drive you . . . it'll be faster and cheaper." He helped her into her coat and led her outside to his car.

After he'd almost carried her inside, he waited in the living room while she got changed into some fresh pyjamas before helping her into bed. He placed a glass of water and a couple of Paracetamol on the bedside table.

"Sleep it off. I'll call you in the morning." He pressed a gentle kiss to her forehead as he placed her phone next to the glass.

Jodie watched James walk out and felt horrible for misleading him the way she had, but it was the only way she could get a bit of time to herself so she could try to think things through. She sipped from the glass of water before grabbing her phone, switching it on, and sending a frantic text to Louise: *I'm fucked.*

Chapter Thirteen: What to Expect When You're Not Expecting . . .

Louise watched as Steve moved around his kitchen with confidence. Now that they were back on speaking terms and more, she could cope with him walking around topless as she watched the muscles shifting under his pale skin.

She'd debated calling in sick to work to allow them uninterrupted time to talk, but she couldn't. She had two new members of staff to train, and her Assistant Manager was due to go on maternity leave. So she had to travel a little further to Steve's flat, where he worked from home doing something with IT support. All she knew was that he had a state-of-the-art computer system set up in the spare room.

Thanks to Jodie's intervention, they had spoken for hours that first afternoon, long into the evening, and had managed to get things straight between them. Once they got past their 'misunderstanding,' they were able to start their relationship from a new beginning with no expectations borne from chance or contrived meetings.

~*~

Jodie didn't want to, but she felt herself pulling back from James after her epiphany had scared the living daylights out of her. It was lucky, for her at least, that he was busy for a couple of days with meetings and deadlines at work, so she wasn't going to be seeing much of him. She was able to fret without having to explain why she paced, chewed her thumbnail, and stressed herself out in general as she thought about things too much.

What she needed was her best friend, a few bottles of wine, and a take-away. Hoping Louise didn't already have plans with Steve, Jodie sent her a text. The response of "Your place or mine" made her smile in relief.

"So, what's wrong?" Louise handed Jodie a carrier bag of steaming curry to plate up. "What with the text last night and then asking for tonight, I know something is giving you the wobbles. Has James fucked you over? If he has—"

Jodie cut her off. "No, he's done nothing. This one is all on me."

They made themselves comfortable at the small kitchen table with their food and large glasses of chilled wine.

Louise could almost hear the gears turning in Jodie's head as she tried to work out how to word what was on her mind. She just waited, eating her food and knowing that if she pushed, she'd only make Jodie more liable to clam up.

"I think I'm in love with James," Jodie blurted out without warning, causing Louise's hand that held her fork to hover inches away from her open mouth. "And it scares the ever-loving shit out of me." After her blunt announcement, Jodie chewed the inside of her cheek while she watched her friend put her fork down, top up both their glasses, take a large mouthful of wine, and look up at her.

"You dippy cow. I thought something was wrong for a minute there." Louise was relieved it wasn't something serious she couldn't help Jodie work through, not that she wouldn't have given it a go, even if it had been.

"This is serious. It's way too soon for me to be thinking this way." Jodie narrowed her eyes at the bark of laughter that was Louise's answer. "It's not funny, Lou."

"It kind of is." Louise held up her hand to stave off the barrage of complaints. "Let me finish before you start. Answer me a few questions, then we'll talk about timing and all that."

"Okay."

"Does James make you feel safe?"

"Yes."

"Does he make you laugh?"

"Yeah."

"Does he listen to what you have to say?"

"Yes."

"Do you miss him when he's not around?"

"Of course."

"Now, this one is the most important. In bed, is it all about him?"

Jodie stared at her.

"I'm serious. Does he just care about his own orgasm, or is it about both of you?"

"I can't believe you."

"Just answer the damn question."

Jodie took a large gulp of wine. "He makes sure both of us . . . er . . . get something out of it."

"Well, seeing as you answered all of those questions in the positive, I would think that it's not too soon for you to be feeling that way about him."

"But we've been together for just a few months."

"So? There's no timeframe set out in stone when it comes to love. If you feel like this, go with it. Don't pull back just because you're afraid. I know you; you're not the type to get devoted just because a member of the opposite sex shows you a bit of attention."

"I . . . just . . . it's . . . Oh, I have no idea."

Louise watched Jodie start to pace around the kitchen trying to gather her thoughts.

~*~*~

16 October 2012- What to Expect When You're Not Expecting. . .

I don't know about you, but when I started serious dating a couple of years ago (before then it had been just casual with the added bonus of getting a shag now and then), I never knew what I was looking for. Was I looking for the next big romance, or was I just looking for more dates? I mean, we date to find a partner, but do we want them to be a life partner or just temporary?

When Paul stood me up, I walked into the pub to have a drink and kill a bit of time, not to meet anyone. I just struck it lucky with James. Even then, after all the "experience" I've had, I didn't expect anything to come from a few hours of flirting and chatting. Yet three months later, we're still spending time together and still enjoying that time.

The magazines all say that the way to find love is to stop looking. I'd always dismissed that as ridiculous and just a backward way to get women like me and Lou to buy more magazines for more advice. I mean, how are you going to find someone to be with if you're not looking?

Men are a little bit like dogs, it would seem, and they can smell desperation. Not a great analogy, I know, but I can say in all honesty

that I met James when I wasn't
looking. He kind of snuck up on me and
wormed his way in. In a good way, of
course.

So the magazines do know what they're
on about. By all means, go out on
dates and try events like speed
dating, but go for the fun and
enjoyment. If you look like you're
having a good time, you give off an
air of confidence, and guys are more
liable to approach you. Who knows, you
might find your James.

~*~*~

Jodie felt a bit stupid as she pressed publish on

the post; she'd never written anything so soppy.

She blamed Louise for getting her to learn to

accept the feelings she had for James. All she had

to do now was tell him.

Chapter Fourteen: Honesty is the Best Policy

Jodie hadn't told anyone other than family and friends that she loved them for such a long time that she wasn't sure how to gauge when the time was right. Should she say it just after sex? Or would that seem too 'caught in the moment?' Should she say it when he arrived at her flat after a trip to wherever for work? It was driving her insane not being able to just say it without having to try and work it into the conversation.

In the end, she decided that she would cook a big meal for James's birthday.

Louise was under orders to bring Steve to join them and ensure the atmosphere was light and fun. Then, they could bugger off home, and Jodie could spill her guts. Yeah, that was going to work to perfection.

~*~

"You don't need to go to all this trouble," James told her as Jodie checked on the vegetables bubbling away on the stove.

"I know I don't, but I want to. Now, you have twenty minutes until Lou and Steve get here, so go and make yourself look pretty." She placed a gentle kiss on the end of his nose and shooed him out of the kitchen.

"I could get used to this bossy side of yours . . ."

She swatted his backside with a metal spoon. "Bugger off and go get changed." She watched his retreating form before checking on the leg of lamb in the oven. Satisfied that everything was going well, she opened a couple of bottles of red wine to allow them to breathe. Just as she finished setting the table that had been dragged into the living room, she heard the door being shut as Louise and Steve let them in.

~*~

"Thank you very much for the gift," James thanked Louise and Steve yet again as they got ready to leave.

"It was nothing. Enjoy the rest of your night." Louise winked at them while Steve helped her put her coat on.

"We will." Jodie kissed her friend, and the men shook hands and made arrangements to meet up for drinks.

At long last, Jodie was alone with the man she loved and was feeling a bit timid.

"Thank you for a wonderful birthday dinner." James gathered her into his arms and peppered her face with wine-scented kisses.

"It was fun. I could get used to playing 'Hostess with the mostest.'" Jodie could feel the effects of the alcohol easing her nerves. "I have another gift for you. I wanted to wait until we were alone before I gave it to you." She led him into the bedroom and made him sit on the end of the bed.

"Is it something that comes in black and slinky?" he asked, a wide grin on his face.

"Not this time, Romeo. It's not much, but I hope you like it." She handed him a small box with trembling hands. She remained standing while he opened it to find a key nestled in shredded tissue paper. He looked up at her, his eyes bright.

"Is this . . .?" He stood up.

"If you want it." Jodie watched him as he attached her spare key to his own key ring.

"I do. Thank you."

"No, thank you." This was it — this was her moment.

"Er . . . why are you thanking me?"

"For talking to me that night in the pub." She sat down before her shaking legs could give out on her. "It was a surprise after being stood up, but it has turned into the best thing to have happened to me in a long time."

"How could I not talk to you? You're gorgeous." Before Jodie could say any more, he claimed her mouth with his. After a while, she had to break the kiss to catch her breath. With her chest heaving, she went in for the kill.

"James, I need you to know . . . I love you."

~*~*~

30 October 2012– Honesty is the Best Policy

Well, she did it. She told him how she felt without throwing up over his shoes or anything like that. I'm so proud of her. When Jodie has her heart set on something, nothing and no one can talk her out of it, so when she decided to throw the dinner party for James's birthday, I went along with her. The fact that she's a brilliant cook had nothing to do with it. I just wanted to help her create the right ambience so she could tell James how she felt about him.

I watched him throughout the evening to try and get a handle on how he would react to the news. All I saw was a man who was smitten with the woman in his life. In fact, I got the feeling that he already loved her. He couldn't take his eyes off her; even when he chatted to Steve, he still kept glancing at her. All I can say is that she deserves every moment of happiness that James brings into her life.

Now, enough about those two, before I start getting cavities from the adorability of their relationship. What is it about unavailable women that attracts men like flies to sh . . . well, you know. Is there a pheromone we release or something that utter arseholes can detect? I've been in an 'official' relationship with Steve for about two weeks. In that time, I have been chatted up by an obscene amount of men, after having spent six months or longer playing the dating game and getting nothing. Unless Jodie and I went somewhere like the speed dating event, nothing. As soon as Steve and I got together . . . BAM!

I've even been contacted out of the blue by guys I dated ages ago. Yeah, like that's ever going to happen. It's the best feeling being able to tell a letch that I am unavailable. It's even better when, as I say that, Steve turns up and wraps me in his arms. Cue a smug grin from me.

All in all, life is feeling pretty good right now. Jodie and I need to discuss what to do with the blog, since we're unsure how much those of you who are still looking will want to hear about how disgustingly happy we are. We'll talk it over and let you guys know what's going to happen, but I just want to thank each and every one of you for reading, commenting, and keeping us going. You are all amazing and deserve to find your own Mister (or Miss) Perfect.

~*~*~

Chapter 15: It's Not Goodbye — It's See You Later

~*~*~

17 November 2012- It's Not Goodbye — It's See You Later

First, I want to apologise for the lack of posts for the last few weeks. Louise and I have been trying to decide what to do with the blog. We were going to just delete it, but after receiving an email from a reader, Steve suggested we pass it on to two readers who are still active in the dating scene.

The email was from Shirley, and she has just met the man of her dreams.

She's been reading the blog for a while but was always too scared to comment. When we posted about going speed dating, she decided to give it a go. She coerced a good friend into going with her, and it was an unmitigated disaster (her words, not mine).

She and her (male) friend ended the night having dinner together, which

114

was nothing new for them. They've been friends for almost twenty years. Anyway, to cut a long story short (and also not to give out too many details about Shirley), the speed dating had made these friends realise the feelings they had for each other . . . feelings they had been ignoring for years.

This was three or four months ago. Last week, he proposed, and they are having a spring wedding. And the best bit? She's invited Louise and me to join them to thank us for playing a part in their happiness.

Note to self: buy a new hat

So what we want our wonderful readers to do is this. If you feel you can continue on with the blog, email us here and explain why you and your friend should be the ones to carry on with it. Think of it as a written audition. The closing date for applications is 1 December 2012, and we will announce the chosen pair on 5 December 2012.

We feel that this is the fairest way that we can pass on what James

```
jokingly calls our "legacy." I hope
you all agree.
```

~*~*~

Jodie grinned at her best friend as they read through the latest post.

"We've done the right thing. I just hope people apply to take over." Louise felt as if she were giving away her first born.

"I'm sure they will, and we'll make sure they're the right ones." Both women had tears in their eyes as Jodie logged off and shut the computer down.

~*~

Louise looked around her empty flat with a smile on her face. She'd never liked living there, which was why she had spent so much time at Jodie's. There had always been a draft, which was great in the summer, but no matter how hard she looked, she'd never been able to find the source.

The neighbours didn't care what state they left the communal areas in, and she hated being so close to the main road. No, she wasn't going to miss it at all.

"That the last of it?" Steve asked her, a bit out of breath from jogging up the four flights of stairs.

"Yeah." She cast one final glance around the empty rooms before grabbing a couple of bin bags, while Steve hefted the last box into his arms. They walked out without a backward glance other than to allow Louise to lock the door and shove the keys back through the letter box.

"Ready?" he asked her.

"More than ready."

They descended the stairs in a comfortable silence and out to the large van, which held the belongings she hadn't sold. They placed the bags and box in the back, climbed into the cab, and drove over to Steve's place. When they arrived, they left the van loaded, Louise felt Steve had earned a reward, and she dragged him into the bedroom.

~*~

Jodie grinned at the text from Louise telling her about the late fee she'd had to pay on the van rental. Her friend's libido was going to get her into trouble one day. She was over the moon that Louise and Steve were still going strong — strong enough for him to cope with her living with him. Jodie knew from experience that Louise's OCD was going to be kicked into overdrive for a while until she settled in and got used to her new surroundings, but Steve had been warned and was willing to take the chance.

They'd handed control of the blog to the new custodians Suzanne and Claire, who seemed to be well-suited to the task. Claire was a journalism student at university, while older sister Suzanne was a copy editor for a small publishing house based in Central London. Both had agreed to allow either Jodie or Louise to post the odd guest post if ever they had something interesting to say. Louise had already written one about "taking the step of moving in with your partner," which had made Jodie and James laugh like hyenas.

James hadn't moved in but spent a lot of time at Jodie's flat. They had talked about it, and rather than invade the other's space, they'd decided that the best thing for them as a couple was to find somewhere new — create their own memories. It didn't scare Jodie as much as she'd expected. Having James by her side every step of the way calmed her nerves so that she was able to see everything from an objective point of view.

They weren't rushing things, wanting to find somewhere perfect for the both of them. The stipulations were that it be close to the airport for

James and close to Steve's flat so that Jodie and Louise could still have their wine-induced girl's nights in. Other than that, it didn't matter as long as they were happy and together.

Putting the finishing touches to her hair and makeup, Jodie walked from her bedroom into the living room where James was checking his email.

"Ready to go?" She stood behind his chair and snaked her arms around his neck, breathing in his scent.

"Yep." James shut the laptop and looked up at her, giving silent thanks to the elusive Paul for standing her up that night. "Where's the gift?" He looked around the room until he found the bright red bag standing next to a bottle of champagne.

"Just be careful you don't drop it." Ever since she'd bought the Bonsai tree, she had gone into protection overdrive.

"It'll be okay. Let's go warm a house." James took her hand and led her out to the waiting taxi.

Epilogue: There's a Light at the End of the Tunnel

~*~*~

14 February 2013 – There's a Light at the End of the Tunnel

I remember that feeling after a crappy date. You know the one: the 'why me' feeling. It's the one you get after the third or fourth consecutive date with a guy (or a girl) who has nothing in common with you, only wants one thing, or is just plain wrong for you on every level.

With the luxury of hindsight, all those bad dates can be construed as practice for the ones that go well. Whether you get a happy ever after out of them or not, they are the reason we stay in the game for so long.

I'm going to tell you something that not many people know. That night in the pub when we first met after Jodie had been stood up by that . . . 'utter fool' is the only way I can describe him . . . I was supposed to be meeting someone myself.

I had been set up on a blind date by my sister-in-law. This girl was supposed to be sweet, pretty, and perfect for me. When Jodie walked in, I hoped she was my date, but there was no emerald pendant on her necklace (how I was to recognise her). My heart dropped, but then I realised I didn't – and still don't – care. I was going to talk to her (Jodie) anyway.

Well, as they say, the rest is history. I don't know if the other girl ever showed up or not. If she did, she never told Nat, or Nat never told me. As horrible as this is going to make me sound, I don't care. I'm glad that Jodie walked in first. If I had already been talking to the other girl, I wouldn't have been able to approach Jodie, and that would have been an utter travesty.

Anyway, enough of the 'might haves' and 'what-ifs.' Things worked out perfectly. I've never been a big believer in fate and all that malarkey, but I often find myself wondering if someone was looking out for us that night. But again, I digress; you may be reading this wondering what the hell is going on.

All I'm doing is rambling, but there is a point to this post, I promise.

Most, if not all, of you know that Jodie and Louise started this blog to document their disappointment with dating in London and to try and impart their learned wisdom garnered through their experiences to others going through the same thing. I'm here to ask the advice of the wonderful readers who love not just Jodie and Lou, but also Suzanne and Claire. With it being

Valentine's Day today, should I do something special, or should I leave it for another day so it's not seen as a bit cheesy?

I'm not going to tell you what I have planned; I just want you to go **HERE** and vote either yes or no. You have until 9pm GMT (it's now 9am) to decide.

Happy voting. - James

~*~*~

"What the hell is that all about?" Louise asked Steve as she closed the laptop.

"I have no idea, babe."

She knew he was lying, but didn't push him. He wouldn't betray someone he now considered one of his closest friends.

"Yeah, sure. I guess I'll have to wait until this evening to find out."

"Yeah, you will. Now leave me to work, woman. Not all of us have the luxury of a day off." He kissed her and turned back to the desk.

~*~

Jodie hadn't had a chance to breathe all day. The acquisition of a new, high profile case necessitated that anything else she was working on be put on the backburner.

She grabbed five minutes to send James a text, letting him know she'd be home an hour late. He replied that it was fine and that he would make sure she had a bath and dinner waiting for her. Smiling, she wondered how she'd ended up being so lucky. James honest-to- God spoiled her, and she couldn't quite work out what she'd done to deserve it. She tried to spoil him back, but he was a man of simple tastes, happy to just curl up together on the sofa and watch a DVD.

Almost two hours later than usual, she shut down her computer and headed out to get the tube home. Due to the time, rush hour was long over, and the underground was quiet. She was able to get a seat for her entire journey, loud music pounding through her headphones to prevent her from falling asleep and missing her stop.

At last, she walked through the front door and kicked off her shoes with a deep sigh. The lights were dimmed, and soft music was playing. She found James in the kitchen humming as he cooked with confidence.

"Bath's just finished running. You have half an hour until the food's ready," he told her with a kiss.

"You are perfect." She walked to the bathroom, shedding her clothes before sinking into the steaming water. Her allotted time was up all too soon, and she was ordered to climb out and get dressed for dinner.

James had gone to town with the low lighting, candles, and atmospheric music — the whole nine yards. Jodie had never seen her living room look so beautiful.

"This is far too much effort." She couldn't help but scold him a little, knowing that he would have spent every minute since he'd finished work preparing their meal.

"Nothing is too much effort. Sit down so I can start to dish up."

Doing as she was told, she sat and pulled the blood-red napkin off her plate to cover her lap. She stared at the set of keys that had been hidden under it.

"What . . . what's this?" She picked them up and looked up at the wide smile on James's face.

"Happy Valentine's Day." He began to serve the delicious meal without giving her any further details.

~*~

Jodie jingled the keys as soon as she finished eating, having been told she had to eat if she wanted to know more. "Are you going to explain these?" It had killed her not to bombard him with questions whilst she ate.

"No, I'm going to show you instead." He took hold of her hand and pulled her to her feet. Then he helped with her coat and led her to the car before driving a short distance through the night toward the outskirts of the borough in which they already lived. After some time, he pulled up outside a low level block of flats and stopped the engine. Jodie climbed out of the car and, nervous, followed him toward the door marked with a large brass "2."

"What are we doing here?"

James just chuckled and indicated that she should unlock the door.

"SURPRISE!" Louise and Steve, clutching a bottle of champagne, appeared in front of her as soon as she flicked the light on.

"What . . . what . . . what is going on?"

James took her into his arms. "I bought us a flat."

She stared at him in disbelief.

"Come and take a look around." He led her by the hand on a tour while Steve popped the cork and poured out four glasses of the ice-cold champagne.

~*~*~

14 February 2013- The Results are in (posted on the 15th)

Well, you voted in your . . . Not quite hundreds, but '"tens" doesn't have the same ring to it. The answer was a resounding "yes," but I think a lot of that was you wanting to know what was happening more than anything else. You bunch of nosey buggers. Well, as I have already done the deed; I guess I should fill you in. No, I didn't propose. I know that's what you were all expecting, but no. I don't think we're quite ready for that yet, but never say never.

I have bought her a house — well, I say house. It's a ground floor, duplex flat. It's the closest we'll get to a house that's a) within our budget, and b) in this area of London.

I hid the keys under her napkin, and after we ate, we drove over to take a look. Of course, Steve and Lou had to be involved in the celebrations and met us there. Lucky for me, Jodie loves it just as much as I do. We had a bit of a party whilst we were there. I can't wait for us to move in and call it our own. I hope this is the beginning of the next stage of our lives together. So, there you go. Our next step? Who knows? Maybe when one of us posts again, it will be another big announcement. You'll just have to wait and see. — James

~*~*~

FIN

About the Author

M. B. Feeney is an army brat who finally settled down in Birmingham, UK with her other half, two kids and a dog. She's also a student teacher, a doodler and a chocoholic. Writing has been her one true love ever since she could spell, and publishing is the culmination of her hard work and ambition.

Signing up with Renaissance Romance Publishing to publish her Novella "Right Click, Love" as part of a compilation in December 2012 is the first step in her writing career that she hopes will span many more works and years.

Her Other Works:

Just Like in the Movies

Honour

Coming Soon:

The One That Got Away

Keep up with her at:

http://mbfeeney.blogspot.com/

Right Click, Love

45267050R00077

Made in the USA
Charleston, SC
18 August 2015